Spin's Really WILD Africa Tour

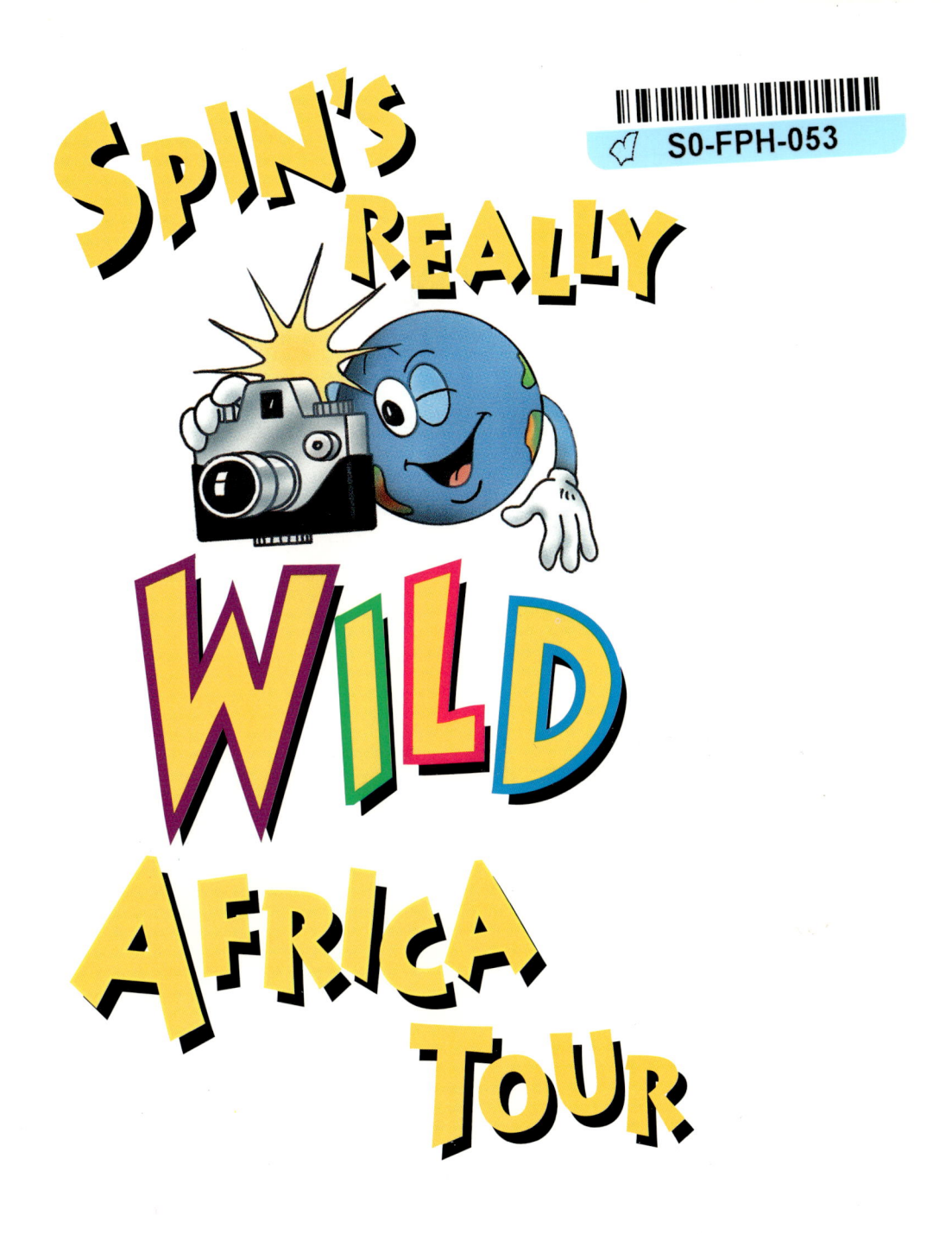

By Jonathan Grupper

NATIONAL GEOGRAPHIC SOCIETY

Washington, D.C.

Hold Tight and Hang Ooooooooh!

Hey, all you swingers out there—
it's me, **SPIN**, your globe on the go.
And here's a really wild riddle for you....

What's furry, friendly, and ferocious all over?

Did you guess Africa?

Then pack up your elephant trunk and grab the nearest vine. We're going on a safari....

AFRICA

EUROPE

ASIA

MEDITERRANEAN SEA

SAHARA

RED SEA

Nile River

Great Rift Valley

Congo River

Virunga Mountains

Masai Mara

Serengeti Plain

GOMBE NATIONAL PARK

ATLANTIC OCEAN

Okavango River

Okavango Delta

ETOSHA NATIONAL PARK

Namib Desert

INDIAN OCEAN

MADAGASCAR

0 Miles 1000
0 Kilometers 1000

SMILE!

On this continent you'll meet the world's **largest, tallest,** and **fastest** land animals.

JACKAL

CHEETAHS

LOOK *SHARP* ALL

GIRAFFES

CROCODILES

YOU MEERKATS ...

AND LOOK OUT!

LION CUBS ARE CUTE AND CURIOUS,
but they grow up to be some of the most fearsome hunters on the Serengeti Plain. What makes them such a roaring success at survival is simple...

TOGETHERNESS!

Lions are the most social of the big cats and live in groups called **prides.** Anywhere from 2 to 15 related females take care of a whole slew of youngsters. A few males, meanwhile, are in charge—until, that is, tougher males turn up to take over.

The name of the game is staying alive, whether you're a predator or its prey. In other words, you're either hunting for your next meal or you're the meal that's being hunted.

The law around here is the

LAW OF SURVIVAL!

There are only **600** or so MOUNTAIN GORILLAS left in the whole world, and they all live in the high, secluded forests of eastern Africa that include the **Virunga Mountains.**

ENDANGERED ANIMAL ALERT!

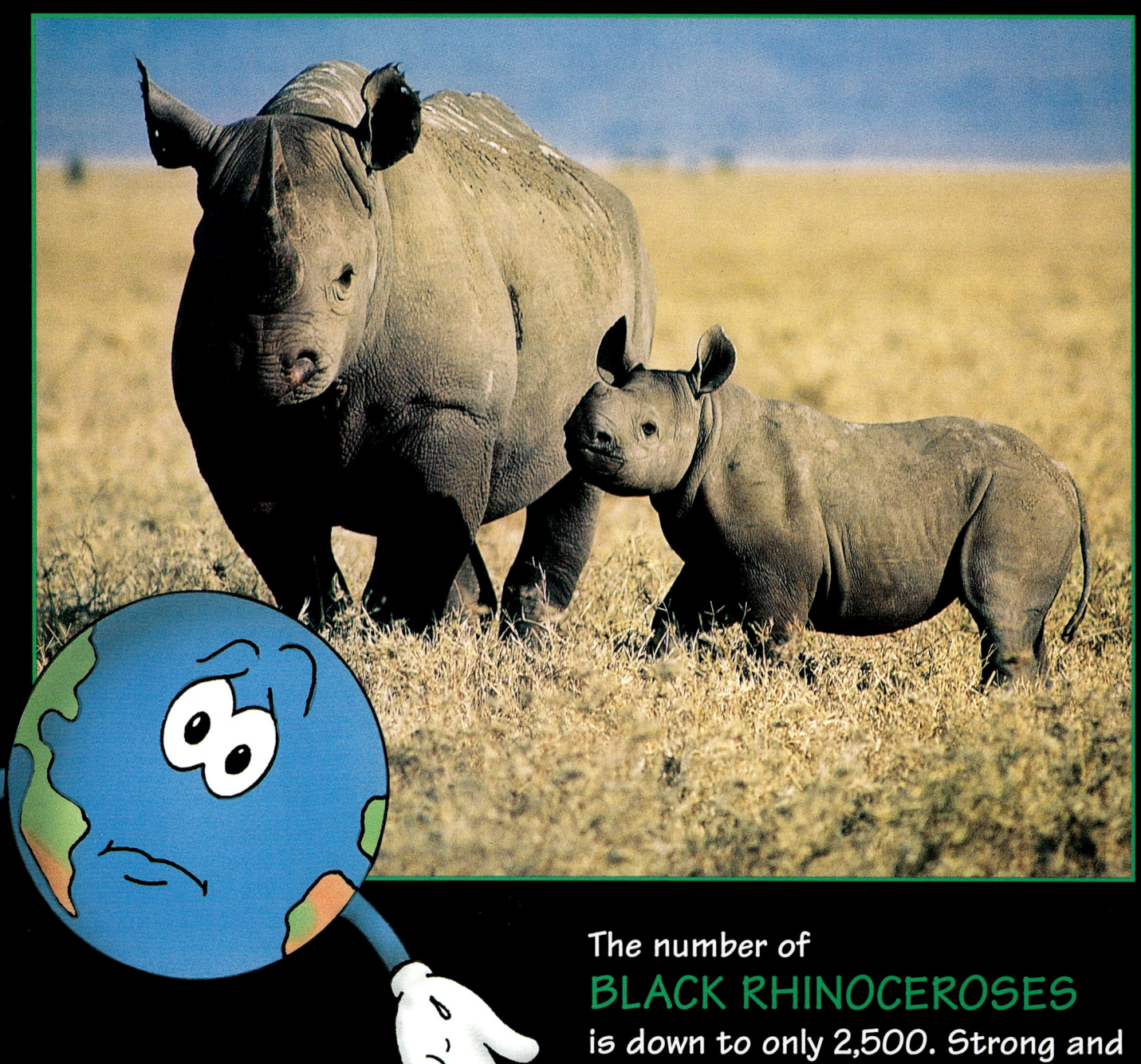

The number of **BLACK RHINOCEROSES** is down to only 2,500. Strong and tough as they seem, they are vulnerable to poachers who kill them for their valuable horns.

What would the world be like if we didn't have Africa's wonderful wildlife?

ID# BATTLE OF THE
COOL CATS

Lions, cheetahs, and leopards all have different approaches to catching prey. Which do you prefer?

STRATEGY

SP

⬆ Sometimes a **LIONESS** will drive her prey into a stampede—straight into the path of a couple of her buddies hiding up ahead in ambush!

STEALTH

The **CHEETAH** relies on speed to chase down a meal. At 60 miles an hour, it's the fastest mammal on land.

EED

The **LEOPARD** lives and hunts alone—and its tactic is sheer surprise. Strong and sly, it may even spring on its prey from a treetop!

Here Today, Gone To... Mara!

The **MASAI MARA**, that is. That's the wide savanna where great herds of **WILDEBEEST** go for months on end during the dry season. Every year, they migrate 800 miles or more.

What makes so much of eastern Africa so lush is its rich volcanic soil. The Masai Mara and the Serengeti are part of the **GREAT RIFT VALLEY**, a vast stretch filled with ancient volcanoes.

Altogether, there are more than a million wildebeest searching for water and fresh grassland. And they're all on the lookout for **predators** like the one on the next page....

YIPES!

MOST WANTED!

NAME: Nile Crocodile
Alias: Smiley

Warning: Suspect is considered armored and dangerous!
Length: Eighteen whopping feet
Weight: Nearly one terrible ton
Profile: Cold-blooded and cool-headed
Last Seen: Grinning, what else?

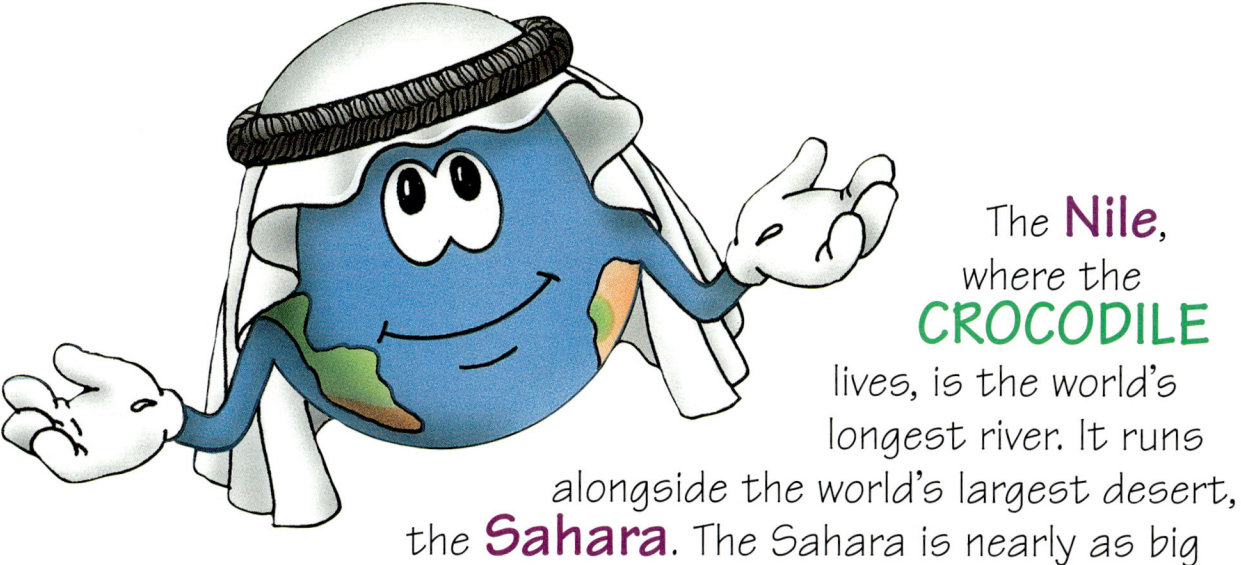

The **Nile**, where the **CROCODILE** lives, is the world's longest river. It runs alongside the world's largest desert, the **Sahara**. The Sahara is nearly as big as the United States. And it's also the toastiest place on earth. Temperatures here once hit 136°F in the shade. Perfect for **CAMELS**.

A camel can slog more than 600 miles without so much as a sip of water.

And when a camel finally does drink, it can chug down as much as 36 gallons in one ten-minute sitting.

STEP LIVELY, HOT FOOT!

The **Namib Desert** in southern Africa has thousand-foot-tall dunes. It gets next to no rain, but now and then a fog rolls in from the sea nearby. So more creatures can live here than in all the earth's deserts combined!

The **SAND-DIVING LIZARD** always keeps a foot or two in the air to stay cool. It slips into the sand to avoid the midday sun.

DUNE BUGGY

This **TENEBRIONID BEETLE** stays perched above the searing sand, thanks to super-long legs. To drink, it tilts its backside against the foggy wind and collects dew drops. These drip down into its mouth.

How's that for table manners?

Now You
Now You Don't!

All over Africa, animals are experts at hiding to avoid predators or to trick prey.

Their colors blend into their surroundings to **CAMOUFLAGE** them. It's the next best thing to **not being there.**

Take a look at how the Namib sands mask a **HORNED ADDER** awaiting its next victim.

Hey, wise guys! What's with the stripes?

No, they're not meant to set a new fashion trend. They help **ZEBRAS** blend together in a group so that enemies can't single them out.

SEE 'EM ...

WELCOME TO HIPPO COUNTRY!

There's nothing like a slurpy mud bath in the **Okavango**. That's the world's largest inland delta, where the Okavango River fans out across a wide stretch of land.

Mud brings out the **HIPPOPOTAMUS** in me. Too bad my eyes and ears aren't smack-dab on top of my head like a hippo's are. That's how a hippo is able to submerge nearly every last inch of its outrageous body—all two sludgy tons of it!

Ahhh...

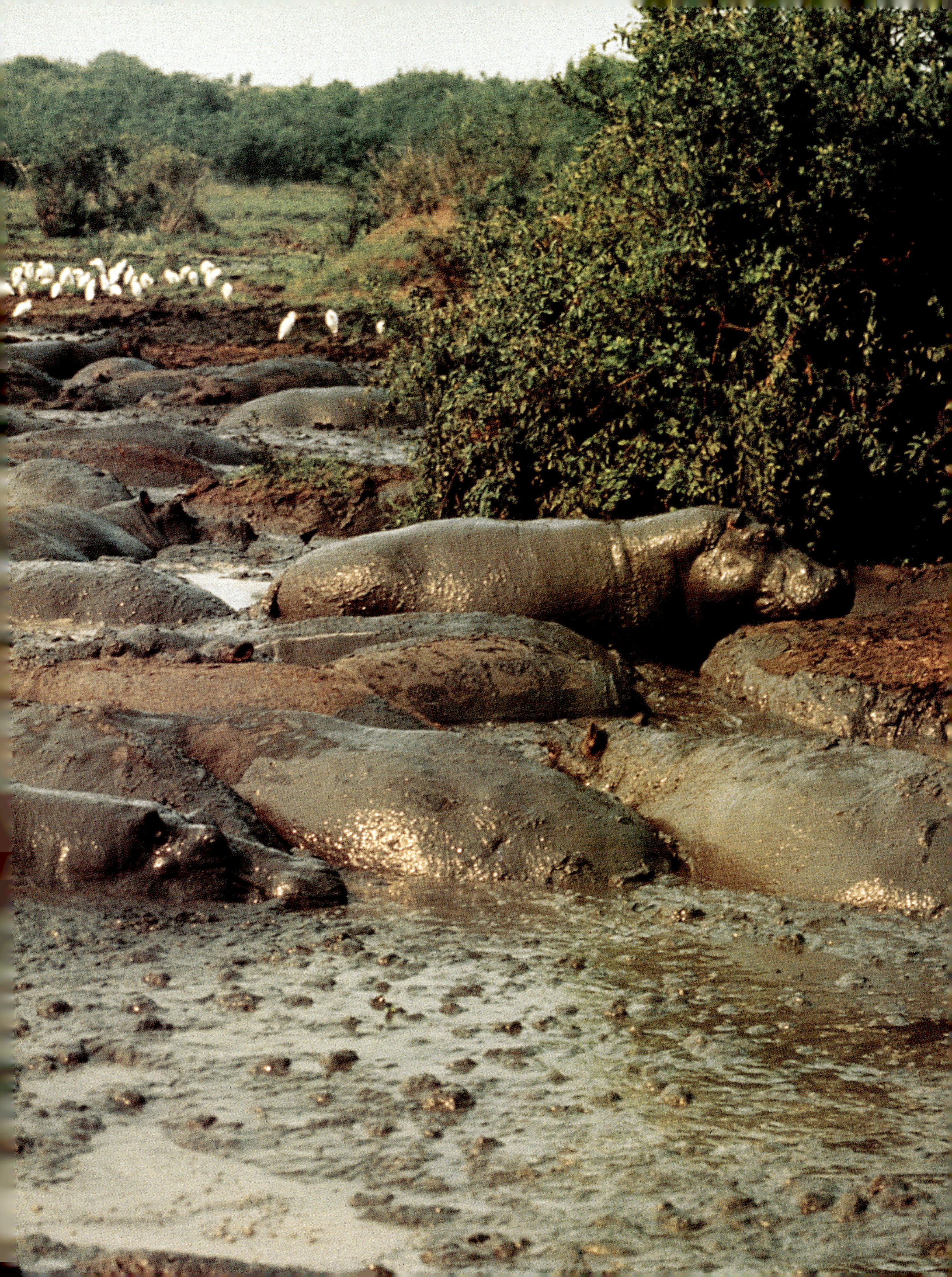

The ELEPHANT makes the hippo look pint-size.
At more than six tons, it's the largest of all land animals.
About 65,000 live in the Okavango—in some of Africa's biggest herds.

Those floppy ears are some of the world's biggest fans—perfect for keeping the big bruisers cool. And an elephant's tusks are part battering ram, part eating utensil, and part shovel.

What about that trunk? It's handy for eating, drinking, hugging, and play-fighting.

Now Here's a Trunk Twister

Say three times fast:

To sip, spar, sniff, SNORT, and snag a leaf aloft
TRUNKS TRULY TRIUMPH!

Like the elephants on the previous page, these two **GIRAFFES** are play-fighting to test each other's strength. It's called "necking!"

Of course, being the **WORLD'S TALLEST ANIMAL** has its drawbacks. Drinking can be a challenge—since the water has to move up six feet or more of throat!

But with their **LONG NECKS,** giraffes can stay on the lookout while others drink. They can also sample those choice morsels in the treetops that nobody else can get near.

One of the giraffe's favorite hangouts is **Etosha**, a vast lake bed in Africa that's bone dry for much of the year.

SURVIVING IS A TALL ORDER!

TASTY TERMITES, COMING RIGHT UP!

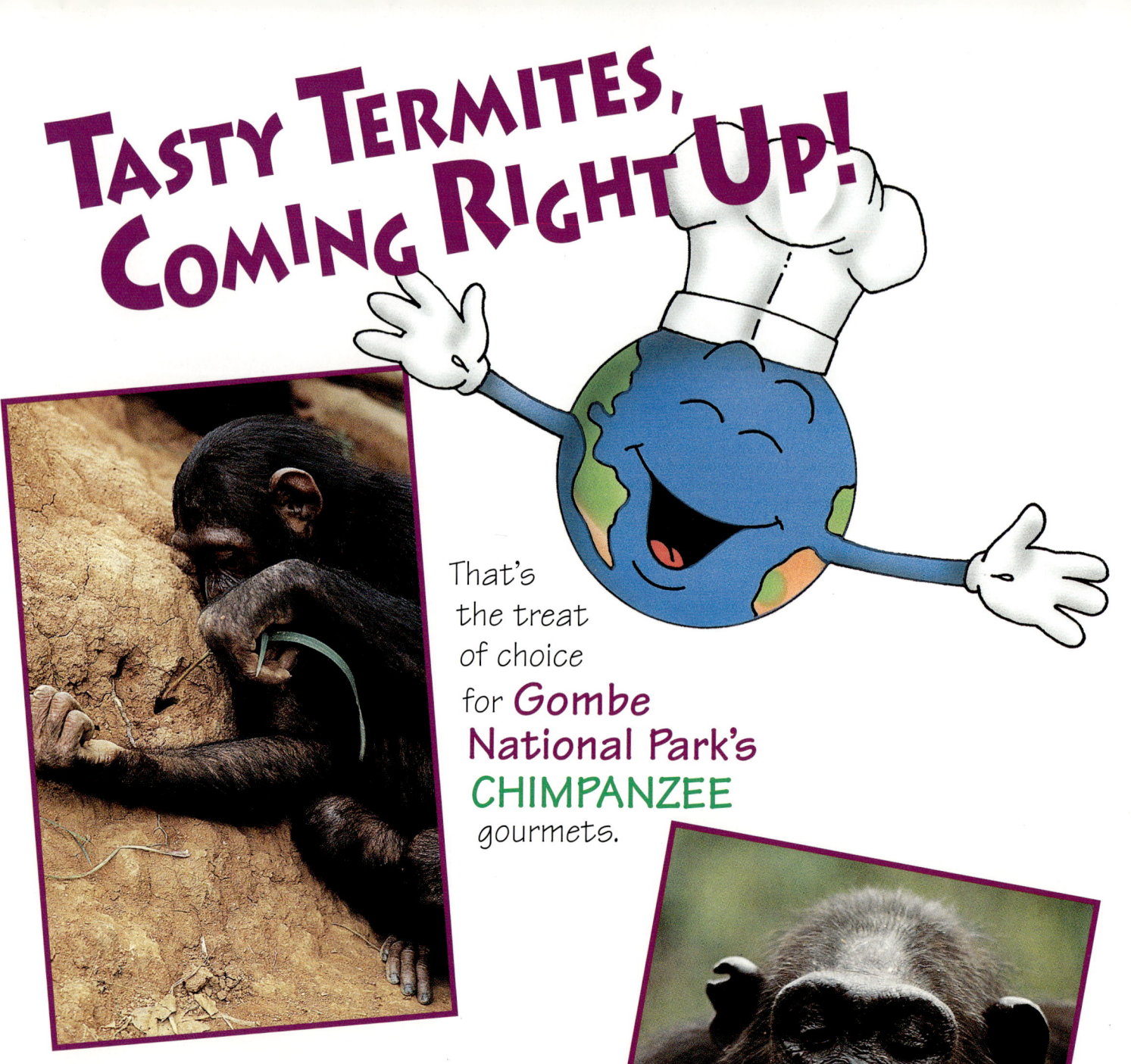

That's the treat of choice for **Gombe National Park's** CHIMPANZEE gourmets.

HERE'S THEIR SECRET RECIPE:

1. **Pluck one** (1) ungarnished blade of grass, twig, or vine.

2. **Dip it into one** (1) delectable termite mound.

3. **Eat one** (1) raw, crunchy termite. Yum! Yum!

Chimpanzees live together in family groups. While dads keep an eye out for danger, moms take charge of the little chimps.
They're PRIMATES, which means they're one of the closest things to humans around!

Hey! Big Bird!

Talk about heads up!
 When it comes to a bird's-eye view, this creature out necks them all.
 The **OSTRICH** is the world's largest bird—and one of the fastest. It runs—not flies—at 45 miles an hour! So a chick has a whole lot of catching up to do. In only six months it will be taller than a man.

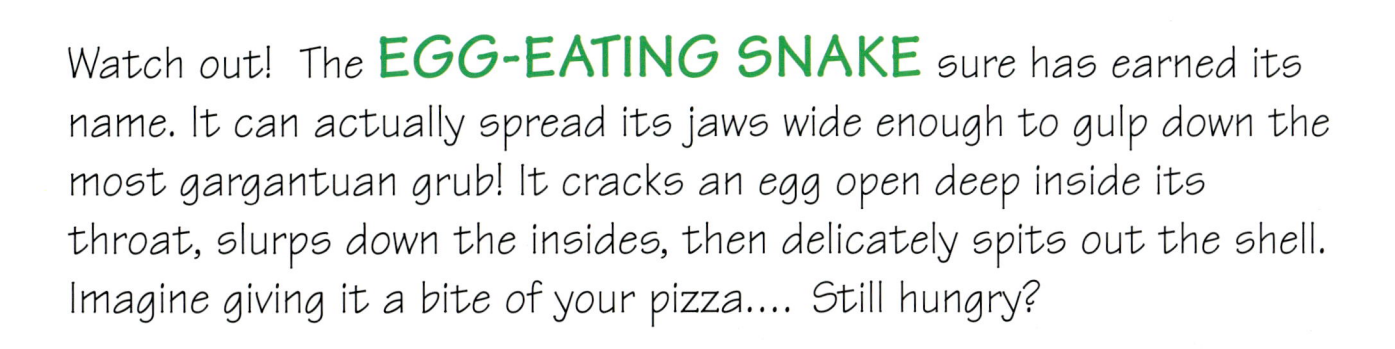

Watch out! The **EGG-EATING SNAKE** sure has earned its name. It can actually spread its jaws wide enough to gulp down the most gargantuan grub! It cracks an egg open deep inside its throat, slurps down the insides, then delicately spits out the shell. Imagine giving it a bite of your pizza.... Still hungry?

WELL, GANG, IT'S BEEN A REALLY WILD SAFARI!

A **SPRINGBOK** *"pronks"* for joy —
and no wonder! From the high mountains, to the
wide savanna, to the hot deserts,
Africa sure is an amazing place to live!

SPIN YOU LATER!

The front cover shows a young chimpanzee in Tanzania.

Published by the National Geographic Society
Gilbert M. Grosvenor, President and Chairman of the Board
Nina D. Hoffman, Senior Vice President

Prepared by the Book Division
William R. Gray, Vice President and Director
Written by Jonathan Grupper • Spin illustrations by Barbara Gibson
Barbara Lalicki, Director of Children's Publishing
Barbara Brownell, Senior editor • Suez Kehl, Art director
Greta Arnold, Illustrations editor • Jennifer L. Burke, Illustrations assistant
Carl Mehler, Map editor • Vincent P. Ryan, Manufacturing manager
Lewis R. Bassford, Production manager

SPIN™ is the host of National Geographic Television's Really Wild Animals™ television and home video series for kids. For information on the videos, call 1-800-343-6610, 8 a.m. to 8 p.m. ET, Monday-Friday.

National Geographic Television
Tim Kelly, President
Andrew Carl Wilk, Executive Producer and Vice President, Programming & Production
Cynthia Van Cleef, Director, Children's Television
Eric R. Meadows, Associate Producer

Photo Credits:
Front Cover: Irven DeVore, Anthro-Photo; page 4 top: Jen and Des Bartlett; pages 4-5 top: Gregory G. Dimijian, M.D.; pages 4-5 bottom: David MacDonald, Oxford Scientific Films Ltd.; page 5 center: Kennan H. Ward; page 5 top right: Jonathan Blair; pages 6-7: Günter Ziesler; page 8: Michael Nichols; page 9: N. Myers, Bruce Coleman Inc.; page 10: Stephen J. Krasemann, DRK; pages 10-11: Yann Arthus-Bertrand, Ardea; page 11: Medford Taylor; pages 12-13: Günter Ziesler; page 14: Frans Lanting, Minden Pictures; page 15: Mickey Gibson, Animals Animals; page 16: David Hughes; pages 16-17: Anthony Bannister; page 17: David Hughes; page 18: Martin Harvey, Australasian Nature Transparencies; page 19: Frans Lanting; pages 20-21 Leonard Lee Rue III; page 22: Jen and Des Bartlett; page 23: William E. Thompson; page 24: Günter Ziesler; page 25: Clem Haagner, Bruce Coleman Inc.; page 26 left: Hugo Van Lawick; page 26 right: Hugo Van Lawick; page 27: Michael Nichols; pages 28-29: Jen and Des Bartlett; page 28 bottom: Jen and Des Bartlett; page 29 left: Michael Fogden; page 29 right: Michael Fogden; pages 30-31: Jen and Des Bartlett.

Copyright © 1996 National Geographic Society.
All rights reserved.
Reproduction of the whole or any part
of the contents without written permission is prohibited.

Library of Congress Catalog Number: 96-14700
ISBN: 0-7922-3501-0

NATIONAL GEOGRAPHIC SOCIETY
1145 17th Street N.W.
Washington, D. C. 20036